Pippen, Scottie.

Reach higher.

15.00
$14.95

35018860

DATE	
	FEB 2 3 2015
	MAR 0 3 2015
	JUN

BAKER & TAYLOR

REACH HIGHER

By Scottie Pippen

with Greg Brown

Illustrations by Doug Keith

Taylor Publishing
Dallas, Texas

Greg Brown has been involved in sports for thirty years as an athlete and award-winning sportswriter. Brown started his Positively For Kids series after being unable to find sports books for his own children that taught life lessons. He is the co-author of *Dan Marino: First and Goal; Kerri Strug: Heart of Gold; Mo Vaughn: Follow Your Dreams; Steve Young: Forever Young; Bonnie Blair: A Winning Edge; Cal Ripken: Count Me In; Troy Aikman: Things Change; Kirby Puckett: Be the Best You Can Be;* and *Edgar Martinez: Patience Pays.* Brown regularly speaks at schools and can be reached at greg@PositivelyForKids.com. He lives in Bothell, Washington, with his wife, Stacy, and two children, Lauren and Benji.

Doug Keith provided the illustrations for the best-selling children's book *Things Change* with Troy Aikman, *Heart of Gold* with Kerri Strug, *Count Me In* with Cal Ripken Jr, and *Forever Young* with Steve Young. His illustrations have appeared in national magazines such as *Sports Illustrated for Kids*, greeting cards, and books. Keith can be reached at his internet address: atozdk@aol.com.

All photos courtesy of Scottie Pippen and his family unless otherwise noted.

Published by Taylor Publishing Company
1550 West Mockingbird Lane
Dallas, Texas 75235

Designed by Steve Willgren

Library of Congress Cataloging-in-Publication Data

Pippen, Scottie.
     Reach higher / by Scottie Pippen with Greg Brown.
         p.   cm.
     Summary: The chicago Bulls basketball star relates the story of his life, including both difficulties and triumphs, in order to encourage readers to persevere as they pursue their dreams.
     ISBN 0-87833-981-7
     1. Pippen, Scottie—Juvenile literature. 2. Basketball players—United States—Biography—Juvenile literature. [1. Pippen, Scottie. 2. Basketball players. 3. Afro-Americans—Biography.] I. Brown, Greg. II. Title.
GV884.P55A3   1997
796.323'092—dc21
[B]
                                          97-3307
                                           CIP
                                         AC

Printed in the United States of America
10 9 8 7 6 5 4 3 2 1

> A portion of this book's proceeds will go to the Scottie Pippen Youth Foundation, which supports a variety of causes for children.

Scottie in his youth.

Hi! I'm Scottie Pippen.

Perhaps you've heard of me because I play in the National Basketball Association.

Perhaps you know of me because I've been part of NBA championship teams with the Chicago Bulls and played on two USA Olympic Dream Teams.

Perhaps you know of me because I've been a longtime teammate of Michael Jordan.

While many people know of me, few know the real me and my true life story. It's a story even I wouldn't believe unless I lived it.

I've written this book to share with you personally some of what I've learned from my successes, as well as my failures, so that you will dare to reach higher in whatever you choose to do in your life.

BILL SMITH

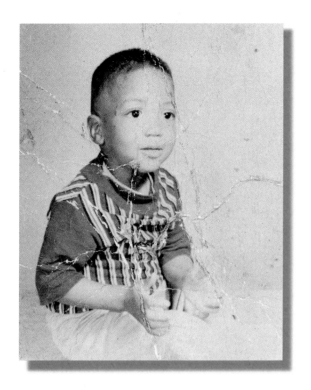

My story begins in a small town in Arkansas called Hamburg. The town of 3,000 people has not grown much since I left. It still has just four stoplights. There are no theaters, not even a McDonald's hamburger in Hamburg. Most in my family still live there.

I was born and raised in the same home. That house started with one bedroom and grew with our family to four rooms by the time I came along. The best addition came when our indoor toilet was installed.

I was the baby of the family, the youngest of 12 children, born September 25, 1965.

Hamburg's town square, 1980

My parents, Preston and Ethel, made the most of the opportunities open to them, which weren't many. They never had a high school education because they worked from an early age to help their families survive the Depression and tough times.

Dad worked various jobs and served in the military. I'm told he was a great baseball player in his prime. But, as a black man in those days, he never had the chance, or hope, of playing Major League baseball.

Dad spent much of his adult life working for a pulp mill in town. Mom worked as a sharecropper, picking cotton, as a child through her teen years. After my parents married, she cleaned homes for extra income.

Some called us poor. I never felt poor.

We never went hungry, thanks to a large garden in our yard.

We lacked money, but we had a rich family, full of love and support.

I'm proud of my parents and their accomplishments. They taught us about faith, honesty, hard work, and discipline.

Preston Pippen

Ethel Pippen

When clothes got too small for me, I'd pass them down to my sisters. Mom would go to the store and buy Scottie some clothes even though he was the smallest. We'd tell Mom she treated him different. She'd say, "Well, he's the baby!" and there was nothing anyone could say.

—Sister Sharon

With six boys and six girls, discipline was an early lesson for all of us Pippens.

Mom and Dad controlled the household. When they said "No!" that was it. You couldn't argue about it. And they would not be embarrassed in public. We couldn't run away from Mom in stores or flop on the ground and cry when we didn't get our way.

Dad could make us stop talking in mid-sentence with just his look. If we were talking in church and he gave us the eye, you knew you better not say another word. My parents instilled a respectful fear in us, which taught us our actions had consequences.

My biggest fear growing up came from hearing sirens. Nobody knows why that scared me so much. Until I went to kindergarten, any time I heard sirens from an ambulance, police car, or fire truck I'd run to an adult and cling to their leg, trembling with fright.

As I grew, so did my responsibilities around the house. I took out the garbage and helped in our family garden.

Homework became my main job. After school, we had to complete our homework before we could play with friends. My parents also made us stay close to home. We couldn't hang out all over town.

Getting my own Western Flier bicycle made my 12th Christmas the best I ever had. I figured a bike would give me freedom to ride away from my parents' strictness. I figured wrong. I could only ride it up and down our front street or around the block.

Despite my parents' watchful eyes, there was plenty of fun to be found in our house. I loved watching my older siblings play sports, and our family watched sports on TV all the time.

I used to play jokes on my brothers at night. I'd sneak up on them in bed and tickle a nose or ear. I'd tease Dad by jumping onto his favorite chair ahead of him and pretending to be asleep. It became a game between us—who'd get the chair first.

Scottie at home with Raye, left, and Dorothy.

Scottie shows his fielding position in the family yard.

Little League baseball became the first organized game I played. I pitched and was a third baseman. I even made the All-Star team.

I had a strong throwing arm thanks to playing catch in our backyard. Dad was already in his 60s and well past his playing days, but I had plenty of brothers to play catch with and close friend Ronnie Martin, who lived nearby.

Scottie, left, with brother Carl.

Years of labor left Dad with painful arthritis. Instead of sitting in Little League stands, Dad would drive his truck to our game and watch from the parking lot.

I didn't realize then how great it was to have Dad watch me play and then talk with him after a game.

I played baseball through junior high, which is where I tried a different sport—football.

Despite being one of the skinniest kids in my class, I played wide receiver.

Scottie wouldn't take any licks in football. If he caught the ball, he'd fall down.
—friend Ronnie Martin

While I enjoyed baseball and football, basketball soon became my sport of choice.

I turned out for our school team when I was 11. I learned the game on concrete at the Pine Street courts in Hamburg.

They are just a few blocks from my parents' home. I have wonderful memories of playing thousands of one-on-one games against my brothers and Ronnie. We pretended to be Magic Johnson, Larry Bird, and Julius Erving (Doctor J).

During drippy summer nights, the bouncing basketball at Pine Street could be heard for miles, well into the dark.

Through junior high and high school, this is where Ronnie and I cemented our friendship and talked about playing in the NBA together. My NBA dream almost ended in high school.

David Moyers

Scottie could barely bench the bar. I used to kid him all the time about that. We'd say, "Look at him, he's so skinny." Of course he had big feet, too. —high school coach Don Wayne

To play basketball for the Hamburg Lions you had to either take a weight training course in the fall or turn out for football. My toothpick body would not have lasted long on the high school field, so my sophomore year I tried weightlifting. I hated it. Coaches and teammates teased me for being a weakling.

My body might have seemed frail, but my desire to play varsity basketball was strong. That made sitting on the bench tough. I felt cob webs forming from spending so much time on the bench my first year in high school.

The highlight of that year came when I dunked for the first time. It happened in warmup drills in practice. Considering I stood only 6-foot-1 then, it showed I had jumping ability (I now have a 48-inch vertical leap).

The frustration of waiting my turn that year faded when tragedy struck our house.

One night at home after dinner, Dad told me to get out of his favorite chair so he could watch TV. Those were his last words. Moments later he suffered a stroke before my eyes. He suddenly slumped unconscious from bleeding in his brain. We frantically called 911.

Dad awoke in a hospital and later came home but never spoke a sentence again. He lived 10 more years in a wheelchair and could say "Yes" and "No." Sometimes he'd mix up the two, so we never knew how much he understood.

Seven years earlier, a freak gym class accident left my brother Ron paralyzed from the neck down when he was in high school. An elbow blow to the back damaged his spine.

Our family's faith told us things happen for a reason—even terribly sad things. We held on tight to that belief even though we didn't understand the reasons. Everyone in town knew about the misfortune of the Pippens.

Scottie (80) poses with Hamburg's football managers, Edward Robertson (11), Aaron Wallace (63) and Nathan Miller (13).

Despite my lack of playing time, I always believed basketball would be part of God's plan for my life. I had visions of playing in college and the NBA.

Those dreams almost never happened because of a decision I made the fall of my junior year. I decided to be the football manager instead of lifting weights with the basketball team.

I loved football and understood the game. I wanted to be part of the team, even if I didn't play. Maybe deep down I saw being manager as the easy way out of weightlifting, too.

I learned the easy way is seldom easier in the long run.

Hamburg High

Since I wasn't on the football team and didn't lift weights, coach Don Wayne kicked me off the basketball team. For weeks we both stood firm in our decisions.

Finally, I realized I had to bow to his rules if I was going to play basketball. Coach Wayne and I had a meeting, and I asked to be allowed back on the team. Coach said I could come back if I agreed to carry out his punishment.

My whole junior season, I'd stay after practice and run up and down about 40 rows of our gym stairs. Ronnie would say, "Go do your job," and wait for me to finish.

That season I swallowed my pride, took my punishment, and still didn't play much in varsity games.

Our parents kept Ronnie and me on a tight leash through high school. We had to be at home by 11:30 on weekend nights. That curfew kept us out of trouble. The only night we didn't make it home on time was when we borrowed my brothers' car and a tire blew out. We put on the spare and it was flat, too. We didn't get home until 4:00 in the morning and had a lot of explaining to do.

Ronnie, senior
year 1984

Scottie, senior
year 1983

David Moyers

David Moyers

> There weren't great expectations for Scottie. He was awful small—just a normal kid. He wasn't the best player on our team.
> —Coach Wayne

The next fall, I lifted weights. As you can see from these pictures, weight training did not pump me up right away.

I entered my senior season standing 6-foot-1, 150 pounds. For the first time, Ronnie, a year younger, and I would play side-by-side as guards. Ronnie was bigger and stronger, and many thought if anyone would make it to the NBA it would be hot-shooting Ronnie.

I knew I needed a big season to get a chance at playing college ball. I did play well and refined my ball-handling skills. But I wasn't flashy. We won our conference championship, and I experienced the joyful tradition of cutting down the nets. We advanced to the state regionals before losing. I made the all-conference team and felt like a special player inside. I guess nobody else saw it, except Coach Wayne.

University of Central Arkansas athletics building and gym.

I graduated from high school in 1983 without a single scholarship offer. No college or junior college coach even invited me to walk-on to their program. Nobody wanted me on their team.

I had my hopes set on two small colleges. I tried out for the Southern Arkansas coaches, but no offer came. I wanted to attend the University of Arkansas at Monticello, where my oldest brother, Billy, went to school. Their basketball coach wasn't interested either.

Our family lived on a fixed income and couldn't afford to send me to college on their own. I needed a scholarship or financial aid.

For months I considered following Dad's steps into the military. One summer phone call from Coach Wayne to his former college coach cracked open a door.

Wayne called University of Central Arkansas coach Don Dyer and told him about me. As a favor to his former player, Dyer offered me a chance.

The deal was this: I'd receive a work-study grant if I agreed to sit out the first year and work in the physical education department as the manager of the basketball team.

I wasn't embarrassed by the offer. When the ball of opportunity rolls by, you have to reach out and grab it. I took the deal and that fall left for UCA, in Conway, Arkansas, about 150 miles from Hamburg.

Turns out several players quit the team that fall of my freshman year, so before the season started Coach Dyer promoted his manager to player. I played in 20 games and averaged 4 points.

I had grown 2 inches since high school and stood 6–3, yet I still had some growing up to do. That spring I skipped classes often and my grades dropped.

The fall of my sophomore year I was suspended from the team because of my poor grades for the first semester. That embarrassment rang like an alarm clock inside of me. I realized I had to change my study habits.

My new dormitory roommate helped too—Ronnie Martin, my longtime friend, earned a basketball scholarship at UCA, and we were once again together.

Ronnie and I pushed each other to improve on the court and in the classroom.

Ronnie and I had great times in college. I continued my practical jokes. My favorite was filling a small trash can of water and leaning it against a dorm neighbor's door.

When the door opened, water spilled into the room. Many in the dorm never knew who did it. Someone did get us back by stinking up our room with cans of sardines in our beds. The key to a good practical joke is to make someone laugh without damaging anything or hurting anyone.

Along with the laughs, Ronnie and I went through some lean times. His family was in the same financial situation as mine. We didn't have much spending money. If I had a few dollars in my pocket, I'd share it with Ronnie, and he'd do the same for me. Many nights we'd go out for something to eat and only have enough money for one hamburger, so we'd cut it in half and share it.

I never shied away from working for extra money. In high school, I worked in a program to repaint the school in the summer. During college I had a busboy job at a restaurant a few months my freshman year. Every summer during my college years I worked. One summer I worked road construction, filling potholes and flagging cars, and once just missed getting hit by a car. I spent several summers welding new school desks together and still have burn marks on my arms as proof.

If professional basketball had not worked out, I might have been a factory manager because I majored in industrial technology. Everyone who plays sports needs a backup plan because there's no guarantee how far you will go or how long your sports career will last. So reach higher inside and outside of sports.

I continued to grow my sophomore year, adding three more inches. That season I stepped up my game as well, averaging 18 points and 10 rebounds.

Thanks to my ball-handling ability from playing guard, I became a versatile player as I grew.

To start my junior season, Coach Dyer asked us to write down our goals on a card. I wrote that my goal was to play in the NBA. It was the first time I told my dream to anyone other than Ronnie.

That year I stood 6–6 and could play all five positions on the court. Coach Dyer demanded we lift weights in the offseason. Instead of fighting it, I realized the extra work would pay off. It did my junior year. My new-found strength helped me play the rough inside game as needed. My scoring improved to 20 points a game with 11 rebounds.

My last inside shot of that 1985–86 season tested my inner strength.

We played Monticello, a school that had rejected me, with a trip to the NAIA national tournament awaiting the winner.

The game went into overtime, and they led by 2 points with time running out. Coach Dyer called for a play to me inside. I put up a bankshot from close range that looked good for a second. The ball bounced off the rim to end our season.

That loss crushed me. Soon, however, that lost chance made me hungrier to work harder.

As I walked through campus, people I passed said, "Hey, Scottie, the team's already left. Man, you missed the bus."

I started to sweat. I didn't have a car for the 3-hour drive. After a few hours of panic, I gave up hope of making the game. I went for some dinner at a favorite restaurant called Chick-a-Dilly. The owner, David Lee, was a big supporter of our team and knew we had a road trip.

"What are you doing here?" he said as soon as I walked in.

I explained the situation, and without thinking he said: "We've got to get you out there to the game."

We jumped into his Cadillac and arrived just before halftime. I suited up during intermission and played in the second half. I think Mr. Lee should have received the game ball from that victory.

By my senior year I had gained more muscle and another inch in height—to 6–7—before I stopped growing.

Two more misses affected my senior season.

During the season I missed a team bus. A class kept me from boarding with my teammates. I went to the gym after class, but the bus went to my dorm to save time and we missed each other.

Coach Dyer couldn't wait and the team left without me.

In my final two years in college, the UCA Bears were 46–12 and won two conference championships. I was twice voted to the NAIA All-America team. I averaged 23 points and 10 rebounds as a senior

All that didn't matter in our final game. Again the winner earned a berth to the small college national tournament.

I figured I needed the exposure of a national tournament for any hopes of making the NBA.

A second straight year, the game came down to my final shot, and again I missed—this one a long-range try as the buzzer sounded. Even though I poured in a career-high 38 points, I felt I lost the game for us.

I melted on the floor in tears.

UCA

> Scottie was one of the smartest players I ever coached. He knew everything happening on the court. The thing about "Pip" is everytime he's had a real opportunity to advance and do something with himself, he's taken advantage of it. —Coach Dyer

Olden Polynice and Scottie.

I felt sorry for myself for a few days after the season ended. Many people gave me needed encouragement, including Coach Dyer, assistant coach Arch Jones, who became a father figure to me, and Ronnie. I was invited to three predraft NBA tryouts to play against the nation's best graduating seniors.

I felt good about myself and what I could do with the basketball. I believed it didn't matter that I came from a small town and a small school. Only talent and my desire mattered.

After the first practice I felt confident. I had solid showings in each tryout and won a dunk contest. The fact that I could dribble, pass, rebound, and shoot suddenly made me a possible first-round draft choice.

Two years before, a guy from a small school in Oklahoma had been drafted by the Detroit Pistons and started making a name for himself. That player who gave me hope that I too could make it in the NBA was Dennis Rodman.

On draft day, the Seattle Sonics drafted me with their first pick, but, by arrangement, immediately traded me to the Chicago Bulls for their first-rounder, Olden Polynice. I knew about the trade before and was excited. Who wouldn't want to play with Michael Jordan?

People always ask me: "What's Michael Jordan like?"

I first met him in a gym before my rookie season. Pete Meyers, who was also from Arkansas and a Bulls player at the time, introduced me.

"So this is your country homeboy?" Michael said to Pete. We talked before playing and hit it off from there.

There's no question Michael is the greatest player I've ever seen. But some people don't understand that even though he's a mega superstar, I'm not awed by him.

I surprised the Bulls coaches and management during my first-year practices when I volunteered to cover him. Many players are intimidated by his talents and mind games. I've always seen him as human. Even when he beat me, I knew I could learn by challenging him.

Michael has taught me so much. He's taught me about being competitive, playing in pain, and reaching down inside yourself in order to reach higher.

People always compare me to Michael, which isn't fair. We have different games. At times I thought I wanted to be like Mike, but after seeing the price he pays for fame I'll stick to being myself.

I've told you part of me likes playing practical jokes, and I've pulled a few on Michael. One thing Michael fears is snakes. So I've placed rubber snakes in his locker to get a laugh. I've also put rats in his dress shoes.

I consider Michael one of my best friends on and off the court.

Michael's stardom took the pressure off me as a first-round pick in my rookie season.

Playing in my first NBA game made me proud and sad at the same time. I wished my parents were there to share it with me. Because of Dad's health, Mom saw me play in college only one time, and Dad had not seen me play since high school.

I sent my parents the videotape of my first NBA game a few days later. Mom says Dad understood. He cried while watching it.

Back pain hampered my first season as I averaged only 8 points a game. Frustration visited me frequently, as trainers couldn't figure out the problem. I had many late-night phone conversations with Ronnie, who led Central Arkansas to the NAIA championship game that year without me.

Back in the 1980s, the Bulls were not as feared as in the 1990s. Chicago had a sorry 20-year

playoff record: No team had advanced past the second round.

When we advanced to the second round my rookie season, a first in seven years for Chicago, it was cause for celebration, even though we lost 1–4 to one of the dominant teams of the time: the Detroit Pistons.

After the season doctors discovered a bulging disc in my spine, and I needed back surgery to fix it. I still suffer backaches at times.

Bill Smith

I missed the first eight games of the next season because of the surgery. When I returned, my slow start drew quick criticism from the media.

I learned fast, whatever you do, don't let people who dog you get you down. I knew inside myself what I could do and that I could take my game higher. I was never satisfied by just being in the NBA. I always wanted to be an All-Star, to win a championship and someday win a Most Valuable Player award.

By the end of that 1988–89 season it seemed my only award would be that of "Scapegoat."

I improved my scoring (14 points a game) and showed my defensive skills (finishing third in the league in steals).

But what most people remember about that season happened in the sixth game of our Eastern Conference Finals with Detroit. We were down 3–2 and needed a win to stay alive. Early in the game, the Pistons' bruising center Bill Laimbeer landed a swift elbow to my head during a rebound. The blow flattened and dazed me. Doctors wouldn't let me return, and we lost to end the season. Some people questioned my toughness.

More people were upset with me by the end of the 1989–90 season.

Again we challenged Detroit in the conference finals, this time pushing the defending NBA champs to a deciding seventh game. During warmups a horrible headache attacked me. It's called a migraine. I felt a pounding hammer on the center of my forehead. My vision blurred and went black around the edges, as if I was going blind. I wanted to throw up.

I had never experienced such a headache. I sat down and tried to shake it, but couldn't. I played the whole game the best I could, scoring only 2 points. You can only give what you've got in any situation. I gave what I could.

People who said I used my headache as an excuse don't know what I went through and don't know me. I have never been afraid of a challenge.

Days later doctors tested me. I feared I had a brain tumor. Thankfully, they found nothing wrong.

To this day I don't know what caused that first migraine and the few that followed. Eye tests showed I needed glasses and wearing them helped. I changed to a better diet with more rest, too.

The stress of losing Dad might have contributed. Dad died during the playoffs that year, and I flew back home between games to be there for his final days. Dad's death has been the toughest loss of all, especially since I never got a chance to tell him how much I loved him and how proud I am of all he accomplished in his life.

Scottie led all scorers with 32 points in the deciding championship game against the Lakers.

Despite the Bulls' lack of playoff accomplishments in my first three seasons, I never got down on myself or our team. We realized we weren't ready to win a championship and needed improvement.

To reach higher you have to believe you are a winner even when you are losing. There's a sports saying: "Some days you get the bear. Some days the bear gets you." That means you have to take the good with the bad. Our turn to win it all came in the 1991 playoffs.

Again we met the Pistons for the conference title, only this time we swept them 4–0. That matched us with the mighty Los Angeles Lakers in the NBA Finals. We lost the first game at home by 2 points, but then won four straight to claim Chicago's first NBA crown. In the last four games, I defended Earvin "Magic" Johnson, the same person I pretended to be back on the Pine Street courts.

Winning a title was wonderful. Playing against Magic was pure magic. It gave me an opportunity to see a dream come true.

AP/Wide World Photos

Scottie's one of my favorite teammates. I've had games when I didn't have a shot for 10-12 minutes. He'd say, "Hey, I'm going to get you a shot." Then he'd pass up a lay-up and kick it out to me. That's what I love about playing with him—he's totally selfless.
—Steve Kerr, Bulls teammate.

For us Bulls and our fans, the dream continued two more years as we beat Portland and Phoenix in the next two championship series.

Our trio of NBA titles made us the first to "threepeat" since the Boston Celtics won eight straight championships from 1959–66.

The elation of our three-year run disappeared just before the start of the next season. Drained by the tragic death of his father, Michael retired from basketball. I was as shocked and saddened as anyone. Later, Michael made a run at playing professional baseball.

The 1993–94 season without Michael proved both satisfying and frustrating. My season statistics were my best ever, and I thought our team played remarkedly well. Horace Grant, B.J. Armstrong, and I made the All-Star team. I had a great game and walked away with the All-Star MVP award. My lowlight came in the second-to-last game of the season.

1994 All-Star MVP

Scottie is the second player in NBA history to lead his team in all major offensive categories for a season. Dave Cowens did it with the Celtics in 1977-78.
Scottie's 1993-94 statistics: 22 points, 8.7 rebounds, 5.6 assists, 2.93 steals.

Tim DeFrisco/Allsport USA

Down 0–2, we needed a victory in Game 3 to stay close in our second-round playoff game with the New York Knicks. The game came down to 1.8 seconds left on the clock with the score tied. Coach Phil Jackson called timeout. He drew a play, which called for rookie Toni Kukoc to receive the ball for the last shot. I was told to in-bound the ball.

In a blink, I made one of the worst decisions of my life. I sat on the bench and refused to go back in. Teammates and coaches screamed at me to play. I just sat there.

It takes courage to stand up, or sit down, for your beliefs. And it takes courage to swallow your pride and go along with the program. The key is having the wisdom to know which is the right thing to do in each situation.

I lacked wisdom that night. I felt disrespected the whole season and had bitterness in my heart. I wasn't against Toni getting the last shot. I just felt at least I deserved to be closer to the basket.

Toni made the game-winning shot anyway (although we lost the series). I apologized to my teammates and coaches after that game.

If I could do it over, I'd go back in the game.

I can think of only two reasons to disobey your coach during a game: 1) If you are asked to hurt someone intentionally; 2) if you are asked to cheat.

Otherwise, you should go along with the plays your coach calls.

I have answered unending questions about those last 1.8 seconds. But if that's my punishment, I'll have to take it.

People sometimes forget that athletes are just like anyone else. We make mistakes; we drop the ball. If we were perfect, we'd make every shot, and not even Michael does that. I know I've missed the mark my share of times on and off the court.

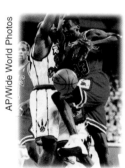

The only thing I can do is learn from my mistakes, ask forgiveness from those I hurt, forgive myself, and move on.

When the criticism has been the worst, my only peace comes from playing basketball. When I'm on the court, my mind lets go of all my worries as I enjoy the game.

As you think about your future, think of the things you enjoy most: those activities and your talents that freeze time and give you peace. Being paid to do what you love is success.

One thing I dread is flying. I sweat almost as much in a plane as on a court. Being in jets scares me every time because of two Bulls flights during the 1994–95 season.

The older jet the Bulls rented once lost power and nose-dived 25,000 feet in about a minute before pulling up. Oxygen masks dropped from the ceiling, and it got so cold you could see your breath. I thought we were going to die as people were saying prayers.

Another time our jet turned hard after takeoff without warning, tossing us around inside. I refused to fly on that jet again and urged the Bulls to change charter companies.

A week later, all of Chicago rejoiced as Michael rejoined the team. I was doubly thankful that week because the Bulls also decided to charter a newer jet.

Michael returned with 17 games left in the season. We made the playoffs, but lost to the Orlando Magic in the second round.

Bill Smith

Nathaniel S. Butler/NBA Photos

Michael and Scottie are the only two players from the same team to be selected to the NBA First Team and All-Defensive Team.

Jonathan Daniel/Allsport USA

That series exposed a team weakness—rebounding. In the offseason, Bulls management asked Michael and me if we wanted Dennis Rodman, one of the best rebounders in history, on our team next season. We both said yes.

I know sometimes there's no explaining Dennis—the different hair colors, the crazy clothes, the outbursts. While I don't always agree with Dennis' style, I don't judge him either.

The addition of Dennis boosted our team to a new level of domination during the 1995–96 season. We became the first NBA team to win 72 games (losing just 10) in a season and then captured our fourth title by beating the pesky Seattle Sonics 4–2 in the finals.

Our season mark and 15–3 playoff record placed us among the best teams in the history of the game.

If you look at that team you'll see a diverse group—different backgrounds, different races, and different nationalities. We all didn't hang out together off the court, yet, for a special season, we worked together on the court to achieve greatness.

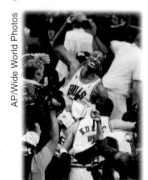

72-10

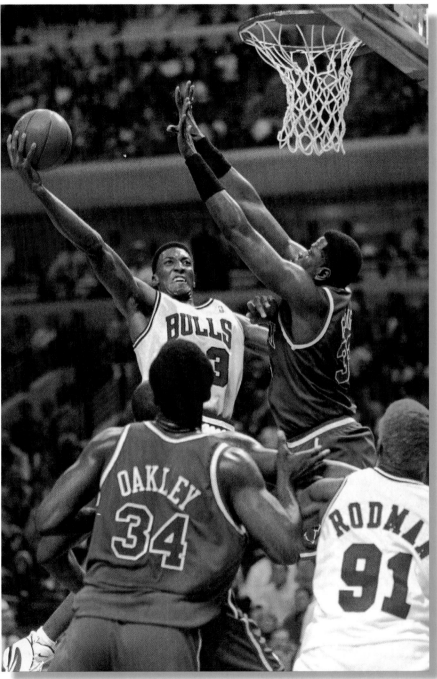

One thing I see hurting the greatness of the game is the savagery of some players.

The game has always had players who talk to each other during the game—challenging, joking, or needling. It's all part of the game's mental battle.

Some of today's trash talking, however, goes out of bounds. Some players are vicious in their verbal and physical attacks.

I don't believe that's what the game is all about. I believe a player can play hard and be physical, play within the rules, and still play with class and dignity.

I've played in more than 900 NBA games, and, so far, I've managed to keep my cool in all but a handful of them.

With people in your face, it's a tough test to stay calm. To be a champion in sports, and life, controlling anger is a must. I've found acting in anger causes more grief than good.

Another reason to control yourself while playing sports is because you represent your family, your community, your school, and sometimes your country.

I've twice had the honor of playing on U.S. Olympic gold-medal basketball teams. The first came in the 1992 Games in Barcelona. We were the first U.S. team comprised of professional players. People called us the Dream Team.

Playing with all the veteran guys, including my childhood heroes Magic and Bird, was another career highlight for me. It was wonderful. The only drawback was we couldn't get out and enjoy the other Olympic competitions much because of our popularity.

When we won the gold medal with an unbeaten record, many eyes were filled with tears of pride.

In the summer of 1996, I had become one of the veterans on the next Dream Team, which featured a younger, more energetic team. We swept through undefeated again, as everyone expected.

A memorable moment came when we met boxing great Muhammad Ali, who stirred emotions by lighting the Olympic flame to open the Atlanta Games.

I looked up to Ali as I grew up. Not only was he champion, but he became ambassador. I've always respected his self-confidence, talent, and convictions.

Reuters/Bettmann

AP/Wide World Photos

Julius Erving (Doctor J) was the player I most wanted to be as a youngster. His high-flying game inspired me.

Dr. Martin Luther King, Jr. is the historical figure I admire most after reading in school about his brave fight for civil rights.

Oprah Winfrey is one of my current heroes. I remember seeing her on TV when she wasn't so famous. I admire her success, passion, and compassion.

Cabrini-Green Tutoring Program

My friend Ronnie Martin is another hero of mine. Ronnie realized after his senior season that his 6–2 height and basketball skills made him a long shot in the pros, so he stuck with college and earned his degree. (I'm taking correspondence courses and hope to graduate in 1998).

Walking away from sports and dreams can tear you up inside. Just as he stuck with me during my down days, I encouraged him when he needed it. Ronnie has a family and lives in Little Rock, Arkansas.

He is a counselor who helps people repair their lives.

We're still close friends and see each other now and then. He helps with summer basketball camps I run in Arkansas for kids as part of my Scottie Pippen Youth Foundation, which has raised more than $800,000 in support of various charities and causes.

I enjoy the time I spend with kids. One program I support in Chicago is the Cabrini-Green Tutoring Program, which helps thousands of students grow

personally and academically. For all of us to reach higher, we must reach out to others.

When I visit kids at Cabrini-Green, I let them see me as a person. I just try to give them hope and tell them about life and what it's been like for me. I tell them basketball wasn't always there for me, how I had to take the time to work at it.

I share how I did the right things my parents asked me to do and stayed out of trouble and in school—the same things I've talked about in this book.

Scottie Pippen has to be considered one of the best all-around players in the game. When one phase of his game is not on key, he's able to contribute in other ways. I think that's the sign of greatness.
—Michael Jordan

AP/Wide World Photos

Andrew D. Bernstein/NBA Photos

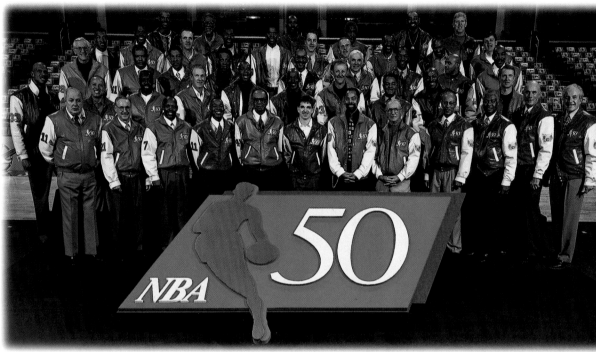

Nathaniel S. Butler/NBA Photo

Following those guidelines to success landed me in honored company during the 1997 All-Star Game in Cleveland.

During halftime, I was introduced, along with 46 others, as one of the top 50 players in the 50-year history of the NBA.

To stand with and be recognized with all the greats of the game created a burst of pride inside me. If you saw me on TV, my smile covered the width of the screen.

It's almost unbelievable to think I was the smallish kid who sat the bench two years in high school, the player no college coach wanted, who agreed to be a manager to get to college.

But everything I've told you is true, thanks to many people who guided and supported me. Always remember you can do great things if you push yourself to reach higher.